Renier-Fréduman Mundil

Allegories

Volume 3

Short Stories

Renier-Fréduman Mundil

Allegories

Volume 3

Short Stories

Translated from German
by Hilary Teske

Bibliographic information from the German National Library:
The German National Library lists this publication in the German National Bibliography; detailed bibliographic data is available online at http://dnb.dnb.de.

Cover design: Dan Winkler
Editing: Malin Friese
Publisher: BoD · Books on Demand GmbH,
Überseering 33, 22297 Hamburg, bod@bod.de
Print: Libri Plureos GmbH,
Friedensallee 273, 22763 Hamburg

ISBN: 978-3-8192-9842-4

For

Viola

Introduction

The allegory is a linguistic placeholder for the parable. To understand a person better, it is worth looking at their whole family. The family member parable has many relatives, obviously close relatives such as mother, father, brother and sister as well as those who have married in from some distant side, adopted, there are also first cousins (first degree) as well as untraceable 25th cousins (25th degree) and probably also a number of family members who are not such - those who simply went to the wedding party, although they had no connection to the family, but pretended to be a deeply connected family member.

A colourful mixture of kinship called allegory, analogy, comparison, simile, didactic piece, metaphor, allegory, similitude, maschal and nimschal and others.

As this picture is very colourful, we can easily imagine that parables not only play a role in the Jewish or Christian religion, but also in many other religions, cultures and poems.

The undisputed grandmaster of the parable is Jesus Christ. He is said to have told (sorry, I haven't counted) 48 parables in the New Testament.

The following is an extract:

- The fig tree (with and without fruit)
- Creditor and two debtors
- House built on rock and sand
- The guest without a wedding garment
- The wise and foolish virgins
- The pearl of great price
- The camel and the eye of the needle
- New wine in old wineskins
- The leavened bread
- The unmerciful creditor
- Treasure in the field
- Mustard seed
- Entrusted talents
- Tares and wheat
- The Last Judgement
- The unjust judge
- The prodigal son
- The lost sheep
- The lost coin
- The Good Samaritan
- The sower

Although Christ used everyday life at that time for his parables - for example, there were no street lamps, everyone walked with an oil lamp, the seed was not sown with millimetre precision using a machine but was scattered by hand, seeds fell on stones, under weeds, etc. - although he used these situations, which we rarely encounter in our everyday lives, they still leave a deep impression today. They are easy to remember with a hidden important message that we discover when we think about them.

One of the things that impressed me was the parable of the five wise and five foolish virgins. All ten waited for the Lord, who did not come at the expected time. When he appeared, the oil lamps were empty. The five wise virgins had a reserve, refilled their lamps and were invited to the wedding feast in heaven. The five foolish ones first had to go to the city to refill their lamps. When they stood at the gates of heaven, these were and remained closed. They were too late, a moment too late because of their negligence, and this brief moment meant that they had to stand outside the locked gates of heaven for an eternity.

This parable reminded me of an incident with my father. We were repairing the drain in the kitchen at home and realised just before we finished that a piece was missing. So we rushed off, ran to the underground, travelled seven stops and rushed to the nearest plumbing shop. Back then, there were no large, almost permanently open DIY shops, and there was no such thing as same-day express delivery via the internet. None of that existed yet.
We arrived at the small shop at exactly 1.01 pm, 1 minute after closing time. Behind the glass pane, we saw the owner locking the door at various levels. We were able to talk to him through the glass door, complaining about our misery, a weekend without normal drainage of the dishwater, no, we would have to dispose of each bowl separately. None of it helped. The owner would not budge. We were standing in front of a closed toilet cubicle for a minute.
That day, there wasn't another young person in the world who understood the five foolish virgins better than I did.
Parables come to life when we look at them through our everyday lives, even if they look

different (but only outwardly) from the time of Christ.

The German word Geglichenes (here translated as allegory) also has relatives: Ausgeglichenes (balance), Abgeglichenes (alignment), Beglichenes (settlement), Verglichenes (comparison) and certainly even more relatives. If we join each of these different family members and look at the parable from the different positions, then a rounded picture emerges from everything, which is what we often strive for in life.

In every parable there is an equation made up of a number of unknowns.

1. OT + NT = BB or
2. OT + NT = L

The first equation is simple:

OT (Old Testament) + **NT** (New Testament) = **B**i**B**le.

But the second equation has another explanation. OT is not only the Old Testament but also Ordinary Times.

O(rdinary)**T**(imes) + **N**(ew) **T**(estament) = **L**ife.

That is the equation behind the parables: the ordinary times links up with the New Testament or the parables so abundant there and results in

(=) life. And which of us doesn't like to understand our complicated lives through this simple equation?

The following collection contains just over 60 short stories, each of which is based on a biblical passage, usually from the New Testament. As we have four children, the stories are deliberately divided into four volumes, a small legacy to the children to discover in their own lives or the lives of their own families the precious treasure of the parables that Christ so often used. A short time to catch your breath, a short time perhaps to reflect, a short time perhaps to delve deeper.

1.
The Golden Dark Neighbor

It was a gray, autumnal day. In the sky, the wind was driving heavy clouds, down on the ground it was whirling up leaves until it was tired of them and heedlessly left them lying. Remnants of fallen leaves clung to the paths, not yet soaked with water from the last rain. Their surface was a slippery sludge.

People hurried through the pedestrian zone towards the covered section of a shopping arcade, seeking shelter from the cold wind. There were benches in front of the stores in the arcade where people could take a break from the stress of shopping. Parents sat together with their children, stuffing their faces with hamburgers and chips, young girls eagerly tucked into sweet scoops of ice cream, boys dug their teeth into kebab sandwiches.

In the middle of the passage, a woman hurried through the hustle and bustle. From time to time, she glanced restlessly, nervously to the side, repeatedly down at her shopping bags, also keeping a constant eye on her handbag. Her breathing was rapid, kilos of groceries hung from her slender hands, bottles rattled against each other in cloth bags, as if to give the woman a bell to make her way through the crowd. Slowly the crowds thinned out, this part of the shopping mall had the most attractive stores, most people were milling around the various stores, only a few were sitting on the benches.

The woman's eyes flickered. Her gait began to sway around a straight line, an imperceptible spin moved the woman's body to the right. She stopped, everything around her began to spin, her body joined the rotation. She tilted violently to the right, gave herself a push in the opposite direction, leaned exuberantly to the opposite side and collapsed to the ground.

Bottles shattered, a red liquid escaped from the cloth bag and spread a sweet, alcoholic scent. It happened right in front of an expensive boutique, the shop windows overloaded with displayed furs, fashionably cut winter collections and handmade leather boots.

The owner stepped outside, having taken in the situation at a glance.

Already drunk in the early morning, he muttered and disappeared back into the store. Shortly afterwards, he reappeared with a broom in his hand. He swept up the food that had fallen out of the bags and pushed it under a bench, not wanting to expose it to the eyes of the distinguished customers.

He looked around briefly in all directions, only a few people were nearby, busy with themselves, not paying attention to him, not paying attention to the woman.

He seized the opportunity, held the broom inconspicuously in front of the woman and pushed the female body behind a flowerpot so that it was no longer in front of the boutique and could no longer be seen from there. Then he turned around and disappeared behind the glittering shop window.

From one moment to the next, the scenario changed. A saleswoman rushed outside from a jewelry store opposite. She looked around briefly, a fraction of a second, but long enough to take in the situation and assess the attention of the few passers-by. The sweet smell of alcohol was still wafting from the polished granite slabs. The woman quickly located the source of the familiar, but at that moment unwelcome, odor.

Next to the entrance door stood a billboard. Golden watches, diamond-studded rings, glittering pearl necklaces were depicted, the billboard cleverly placed in the passageway so that it automatically drew some of the stream of passers-by into the store.

With a quick movement, the woman turned the billboard and pushed it in front of the reclining female body, from whose proximity the alcohol vapor was still rising. The reclining human form was now squeezed between the flowerpots and advertisements, displaced by a ghostly hand, barely visible to the shoppers on either side of the stores.

The flowerpots were surrounded by benches, an artificial oasis of calm in the hustle and bustle. A corpulent mother, holding a seven-year-old girl by the hand, placed her massive body on the wooden surface. The fat woman's body was already dressed in winter clothes, here in the covered, heated passageway, her body was sweating and expelling the excess heat with panting breath.

Someone is lying there, said the child.

The mother did not react.

A woman is lying by the flowers...

Now the woman turned around and discovered the prostrate human being for herself. Most of the scent of the cloud of alcohol had evaporated, but the woman had a fine, culinary nose and noticed the scant remains.

I'll buy you an ice cream, she said curtly and stood up.

Is the woman asleep?

The mother nodded.

Then we'll have to cover her up.

No, it's nice and warm in here.

And if she's not asleep? Then why is she lying here?

She's asleep, you don't understand that yet.

What do you mean?

Some people sleep outside. They just want to. And now stop chattering.

They both walked in silence to the nearest ice cream parlor.

Oh my goodness, the man burst out, what's wrong with you?

He was tall and strong, broad shoulders, his thick hair braided into ringlets, colorful clothes clinging to his black skin. The man pushed the advertising wall aside and knelt down next to the prostrate woman.

Is there something wrong, madam?

The woman opened her eyes, one of which opened just a crack. Her speech consisted of slurred words, barely understandable. She tried to reach for her handbag, but her arm wouldn't obey her.

Stay calm, said the man in a low, gentle stream of speech. Stay calm, I'll take care of you.

He lifted the woman onto his shoulders, straightened up and hurried through the passage. After 50 meters he passed drunken men, their hair cut extremely short. He immediately caught their eyes.

Keep your dirty hands off the woman, one of them shouted at him.

At the same time, he loosened the leash in his hand, at the end of which a dog was crouching. Growling, the animal leapt forward. Undeterred, the black body hurried on, spotting the sign of a doctor's surgery ahead. His steps quickened, he ran when he reached the stairs, hurried up the steps and rushed into the surgery.

The receptionist immediately recognized the situation.

Follow me, she ordered and hurried into a treatment room. Put the woman on the couch and I'll call the doctor.

The rest took its predetermined course.

Probably a stroke, the doctor said to his assistant, call an ambulance.

Is there anything else I can do? asked the black man.

Do you know the woman? the doctor asked.

No, she was lying in the shopping mall.

We need to find out her name.

Here's her ID, I found it in her bag.

That was very circumspect of you, said the doctor, threading a cannula into the crook of the woman's arm with a firm grip.

The dark-skinned man turned around and left the surgery. He had to get back, even if it meant walking past the dog, the drunk and the men with short cropped hair again.

Once at the square, he gathered up the things scattered among the flower pots. He searched through the bags and found nothing but the woman's name, no address, no telephone number.

He reached for his cell phone, he still had a few euros credit on his SIM card. The call to directory enquiries was damned expensive, the credit ran out like sand between his fingers. After the woman had given the address and was about to add the phone number, the connection broke off. The card was empty.
The man knew the address. He loaded his arms with the bags and set off, passing the men with short cropped hair a third time. After half an hour, he reached the house he was looking for. When he rang the doorbell, a well-dressed gentleman appeared.
The stranger explained what had happened and handed him the bags.

How can I thank you, can I do anything for you?

No, the black man shook his head, I have everything I need. Even a cell phone. And an empty wallet. He didn't mention it or the fact that he was only tolerated in this country.

Really nothing, sir, I'm happy. But if you ever find me on the ground between the flowerpots, please pick me up. You can do that for me.

When the man heard this, he went back into the house sadly, for he had never touched a black man before.

Which one of these do you think turned out to be the closest to the one who fell to the ground?

The one who picked her up.

Then go, and act the same way.

So whatever you expect of others, do to them! This is the law and the prophets.
(Matthew 7:12)

When the young man heard this, he went away sorrowful, for he had a great fortune.
(Matthew 19:22)

2.
Debtor Domino

Outside, on the road trees, road markings, crash barriers and the shadows of animals rushed past. An hour, another hour. It had been three days. And now just another hour. Would much have changed? Hardly. Everything would be like the last time. No, better, more intense. Soak up every moment of the coming night. Memories in anticipation of the next three days, until the next night came.

His foot pressed the gas pedal harder. Beneath his body, the car jerked, accelerated and shot forward. The shadows of the animals merged into a black wall, interspersed with the dark pillars of the trees. Everything was like a foreboding dream. Only rarely did he overtake another car drifting heedlessly through the night. Now he was almost alone, alone with himself, the night and his expectations. He surrendered to his thoughts, they were far away, no longer in the car itself, somewhere up ahead already.

The engine was running quietly and evenly over the night-saturated asphalt, driving the wheels through time as if it were a matter of getting hold of a blue ribbon for the fastest crossing of the highway.

Unexpectedly, the steady rhythm changed, at first barely noticeable, then more violent. Lights began to flash on the dashboard, bright, dark red like spilled blood. For a few minutes, he let himself be driven forward by the inertia of the propelled mass, then he finally realized that it was pointless.

His damp hands pulled the steering wheel to the right, he tapped the hazard lights with his little finger and let the car coast down the hard shoulder. He knew that he knew nothing about cars, engines, electronics and tangled cables. Nevertheless, he got out and lifted the hood. In front of him was an unbearable mystery of electricity and mechanics, allied with the night, against him, against his expectations of the future.

He stood outside next to the car, dimly lit by the hazard lights, and waited. The few cars he had recently overtaken drove past his distress indifferently.

Maybe they didn't see me, he thought, maybe one or two of the drivers had fallen asleep and the cars were rolling through time without a driver. From behind, he heard a loud humming noise, obviously a larger car was approaching. He soon recognized the car of a breakdown service. Fate was kind to him. He raised the warning light high in anticipation and waved it violently in front of his chest. As the car passed, all he could see was the driver's face; at the same moment, the light on the roof of the service car went out, signaling that he had just come off duty.

A few more cars rolled past him, even an empty tow truck. They didn't even slow down; suddenly, just as they had appeared, they disappeared into nothingness.

He must have been sitting in the car for half an hour and had dozed off for a few moments when a loud honk startled him. Shortly afterwards, a man was standing next to the car door. His face was unshaven, his hair knotted into a ponytail, worn jeans over his legs, his upper body casual in a loose shirt hanging over his trousers.

Why couldn't a person walk through life as decently as he did, he thought. This guy was probably a long-term student, living a comfortable life at the expense of his taxes, perhaps also a welfare recipient, traveling happily through life while others toiled away.

He gulped. Necessity evened things out.

Do you know anything about cars? he answered reluctantly.

Open the hood.

The young man's head disappeared into the engine block, his hands rummaged through the thicket of cables, his slender fingers gliding lovingly over the warm innards of the car.

Everything seemed to be in order. In any case, neither the eyes nor the sense of touch of the fingers had reported a mistake. Once again, deeper than before, the young man's body disappeared, his strained breathing rose into the black night, the movements of his hands became stronger, they moved unerringly over the parts that had already been scanned a second time.

Try to start the engine!

Nothing happened.

I thought so, said the young man. But you're lucky.

Why is that?

I know what the problem is. We need to replace a part.

You have a sense of humor. How do we get hold of a spare part?

Not at all. I don't mean what you think. I'll take the part out of my car and put it in yours.

You'll what? he asked in astonishment.

You heard me right. Your luck is that I live very close by. The road goes downhill from here for five kilometers. I'll let my car roll down the hard shoulder to the next exit. From there it's only a few minutes' walk home. I can sort it out tomorrow.

I can't expect you to do that.

You don't have to either. I'll do it anyway.

After ten minutes, the replacement was finished. The young man fetched his spare canister.

You'll need it. Your tank is pretty empty, you might not make it to the next gas pump.

He wanted to give him money, asked for his address and phone number, but the young man just waved him off. As he said goodbye, he saw open books on the passenger seat.

I have an exam tomorrow, said the young man, explaining. I actually wanted to study a bit more. But I'll be fine.

They parted company. He watched the old car roll leisurely down the hill on the hard shoulder, then started the engine and sped off into the night, towards his expectations. They were female, ten years younger than him, like in a trashy novel: blue eyes framed by long blonde hair. Exactly the opposite of his wife, everything he had been missing for the last few years.

The night belonged to the two of them. He stepped on the gas pedal to make up for lost time.

After fifteen minutes, he saw a flashing warning light on the side of the road from a distance. He had already left the highway and was driving along a narrow country road. As he approached, he recognized the desperate face of a woman. Her trembling revealed that she had been holding out in the cold night for some time. He glanced at his watch.

He had wanted to be with her for an hour, to hold her in his arms, to share the night with her. He didn't even blink as he rushed past the strange woman. He didn't know anything about cars anyway, and he was a polite, correct man who had had a date an hour ago.

How was he supposed to know that the husband of the woman standing on the side of the road had been admitted to hospital as an emergency case? Perhaps she wouldn't even see him alive one last time.

Everyone had their own fate. Slowly, the image of the woman froze in the glow of the steadily receding rear lights of his car.

Therefore, the kingdom of heaven is like a king who wanted to settle accounts with his servants. As he began the settlement, a man who owed him ten thousand bags of gold was brought to him. Since he was not able to pay, the master ordered that he and his wife and his children and all that he had be sold to repay the debt. At this the servant fell on his knees before him. 'Be patient with me,' he begged, 'and I will pay back everything.' The servant's master took pity on him, canceled the debt and let him go.

But when that servant went out, he found one of his fellow servants who owed him a hundred silver coins. He grabbed him and began to choke him. 'Pay back what you owe me!' he demanded. His fellow servant fell to his knees and begged

him, 'Be patient with me, and I will pay it back.' But he refused. Instead, he went off and had the man thrown into prison until he could pay the debt. When the other servants saw what had happened, they were outraged and went and told their master everything that had happened.
(Matthew 18:23-30)

3.
Managed Services

He sat in his wide leather armchair, the expanse of a massive mahogany desk opened up in front of him, easily accommodating 20 people. Behind him was a full-length glass wall that offered a view of the city below. A metropolis of four million people lay at his feet. There was hardly a street where he didn't earn money with his business. The lights of the cars were like twinkling stars in the night.

He must have dozed off in between. The clock said 4:00 at night. It had been a long time since his working hours had ended so late. Years, many years ago, he started the business, it shot out of the ground like a mushroom cloud, soon the infectious cloud lay over the whole city. Somehow he had managed to transfer the idea of discount stores to the cleaning industry.

Not only was it cheap, it was also good. Quality was one reason for his success. Good and cheap, a golden road, certainly not easy to travel for his employees, a road cut through the jungle of

human habits and expectations. Good and cheap, he thought, but it wasn't enough.
Others were also good and cheap. The price could no longer be lowered at will. So something else had to be added. The idea came to him at a discount grocery store. Not only was there butter, milk, cheese and bread, there were also shirts, bicycles, writing pads and computers. He had to combine good and cheap with something else, something not normally expected in the cleaning industry.
So he offered an all-round service. Cleaning work was the basic service, the food in the discount store. Anyone who wanted to, could book any additional service. All his cleaning women, sorry, cleaning ladies, had a second qualification. Some were perfect babysitters, others were excellent cooks, some were sufficiently fast at typing, there were cleaners with basic nursing skills, and, and, and.
The customer could book a cleaner with him, who would stay an extra two hours to look after the children, spend an hour at the typewriter typing unfinished letters, who would jet around the Internet after cleaning the office, looking up

the cheapest flights for the next week for the office staff.

Suddenly the phone rang. He was startled. 04:00 in the morning, who was calling him? His wife?

Wegel & Co KG Cleaning and Services, what can I do for you?

I can't do it today, the voice on the other end faltered. I'm exhausted.

A quiet sob could be heard. As he knew his company inside out, he understood the situation immediately. His industry was a 24-hour operation. The switchboard was always manned to organize a replacement if someone called in sick.

What's the problem? he asked back.

The time, replied the woman at the other end. There's a rule. You know that. You have to call in sick no later than one hour after starting work.

That's sensible, he said. A replacement, we have to get a replacement. When were you supposed to start?

At 2:30.

2:30 a.m., he burst out, where on earth do you go cleaning at 2:30 a.m.?

In the office building on Lake Ligulen. After that, I have to go to a nursing home for another two hours to scrub the bathrooms before the old people are scrubbed down themselves.

You've got a problem there, he replied. You are calling in sick half an hour late.

Couldn't you, the other voice faltered, couldn't you say I called at 03:10?

Now he fully realized his situation. The employee at the switchboard had, probably by mistake, diverted the phone line to his office. He had to identify himself or slip into the role of receptionist.

How do you imagine that would work? I can't get a replacement in this short time. They'll blame me. They'll say 03:10 to me, the ones from HR, they'll say 03:10 with relish and then look me in the eye and ask why I didn't bring in a replacement. I would have had enough time.

Then they'll fire me, the woman's voice faltered. They will do it, I know it.

There was a long pause, for many moments he didn't know whether the woman was still on the phone.

Don't worry, he said suddenly. I think I can manage to solve our problem. Now tell me your name first.

Mary, Mary McNorton.

Good, I've made a note of it. How long do you think you'll be ill?

I don't know. Maybe a week, I'm completely exhausted. The woman's voice began to sob again.

A week, first of all a week, he repeated. I've made a note of it and will pass it on to the HR department.

Thank you, thank you very much, said the woman on the other end. I was lucky you were on duty today.

That's all right. We have to finish now so that I can get everything in order.

When the conversation was over, he hastily switched on his PC and sent an e-mail to the HR department with a different sender.

Mary McNorton called at 03:10 today to say she was ill. It is expected to last a week. A replacement has been arranged.

Then he got up and went to a corner of the huge office where there was an old spin. The first one he had bought, in which he kept his last work things. He took the work overalls and the bucket of cleaning products and made his way to the tower block in Ligulenweg. When he had finished, he hurried to the nursing home, where he was impatiently awaited. The reception was not very friendly because he was late.

Hurry up, the nurse urged him. We've also booked you for the meal today.

The meal? he repeated.

Yes, didn't they tell you? Someone from the morning shift has dropped out. Two hours of help with breakfast. We booked it with your company at short notice.

Oh yes, sorry, I forgot for a moment.

After he had finished with the baths, tired and weary, sweaty, they put him in a nursing gown. The food had already been served.

Go to room 20, the woman at the window needs to be fed. And then to room 25, the new arrival in the middle, the same as in room 20. Ten minutes, you understand, 10 minutes maximum for each of them.

He hurried into the first room and recognized an emaciated figure in the pale morning light. The woman reminded him of his mother, but his mother had been dead for ten years. He

carefully straightened up the old body and fed her breakfast.
Each bite took an eternity, old, faded eyes looked at him while the teeth underneath slowly ground the bread.

I was sick, and you visited me; I was in prison, and you came to me. For I was hungry, and you gave me food; I was thirsty, and you gave me drink. (Matthew 25:35-36)
The morning had already begun, the offices of the HR department were starting to fill up. Ms. Tort, the HR manager, was checking her e-mails, all sick notes had to go through her desk, everything that meant power over others she grabbed with her greedy, shaky, blind hands.

This Mary McNorton, she said to her secretary, she was lucky once again. But I don't trust it. Have the switchboard check who was on duty tonight and when the call was actually received.
The old woman lay back down, exhausted from breakfast. He hurried into room 25, the new arrival in the middle. His schedule was way behind.

When did we see you sick or in prison and come to see you? When did we see you hungry and fed you, or thirsty and gave you something to drink? (Matthew 25:37-39)

While he was taking care of the new arrival, the personnel manager's secretary ran to the switchboard.

Mary McNorton was asleep again, weary and exhausted, feverish, she slipped into a nightmare.

He had managed everything well. The office building. The nursing home bathrooms. And the two extra hours of care. Mary McNorton didn't need to worry, he'd found a replacement in time.

Amen, I say to you. Whatever you have done for one of the least of these, you have done it unto me. (Matthew 25:40)

4.
The Glass Fist

Under the glass top of the table, his hand clenched into a fist. The claw of a black raven, digging into an invisible enemy. The enemy? Wasn't everyone the enemy of everyone else, sometimes you were even your own enemy. The enemy was gone, therefore invisible, yet only more real in his memory, hatred turned into an image, covered in anger, rage, soled with curses, protected – his head covered – with the veil of uncontrolled emotions.

Once again he reached for the paper, the old page from the application section of a newspaper. At that moment, he had immediately sensed that this was his big chance. Just a small advertisement, not lavishly laid out, brimming with simplicity, probably trusting that the simple layout would attract the right people.

- Alternative to office work - personal secretary sought -

That was all the advertisement had said. The days of hiring personal secretaries were long

gone. Who could still afford it? And if so, such a post was usually given to confidants, acquaint-tances, family members, close colleagues.
An alternative to daily office work, he repeated in his mind. No getting up early every day, the same stink five times a week, no annoying office desk, no office cage in the middle of the noisy city.
In the middle of the city. He bit his tongue. The place of work of the secretary being sought was a Spanish Balearic Island. Three months in England in the summer, one month in Switzerland in the winter, the rest of the time Spain, sun, water, Balearics.
He tried to calm himself down. How could he possibly have been sure that he would have got the job? Nonsense. A futile attempt at distraction. Of course he could be sure. His application had met with an unexpectedly positive response. They had got on extremely well during the interview. He already had a verbal acceptance in his pocket. Or rather, in his ear. Then the delay. The old lady, his future boss, had fallen ill at short notice. Three weeks in hospital, nothing serious, but three weeks can change a lot.

During this time, he had been careless, careless after a year of unemployment, during these three weeks his old friend Ben had turned up. Why, actually? He didn't know. He remembered the meeting in the café as if it had just happened. Suddenly they had talked about plans for the future. He suddenly started talking about his future job. Of course, he was clever enough not to reveal the old lady's name or address.

Ben had found it out. It could only have happened in the short time he went to the toilet. His jacket was hanging over the chair, with his wallet, containing the name, telephone number, address, even the advertisement with box number. Ben must have been nosing around in his wallet during this time. It was only afterwards that he realized that the notes were in a different order in the black leather wallet. He had looked at them several times a day. When you're out of work for a year, you learn to pay attention to every little thing.

He had enquired about the old lady in hospital. She was due to stay for at least another two weeks and he used the time for a short trip – from the rest of his savings. Soon there would

be a rich source of money flowing in every month. Soon.
Ben was his enemy, wasn't he? He was a sneaky, vile, parasitic pig, the epitome of a parasite, who even feasted on the coagulated blood of the corpses that littered his path through life.
When he returned from his journey, he found the letter. From the old lady. The confirmation. He rubbed his hands together, curious about the details.

Dear...
My recent illness has forced me to reconsider my situation. The circumstances that have arisen have forced me to abandon my original intention. My business situation has prompted me to give preference to another applicant. In addition to having the same excellent qualifications as you, he has basic medical training, which gives me an additional sense of security. I very much regret not being able to give you any other final information and hope for your understanding. Given your excellent qualifications, I am sure that you will soon find a similar suitable position.

He had to laugh. It was as if someone had picked six numbers in the lottery after twenty years, couldn't find the ticket and someone tried to comfort him by saying: no problem, next week you'll pick six again.
He knew immediately that Ben was the other one. Ben was now the personal secretary of a wealthy old lady who lived on a stately estate on a Spanish Balearic island. But that was not all. He owned his own house on the sprawling estate and, as the old lady was childless and no longer had any relatives, this Ben had been included in significant parts of the will.
Now, after five years, five years that meant going to an office day in, day out in the stuffy city, not to mention the arduous journeys, overcrowded stuffy trains, past alcohol-soaked bodies lying there at night and the many new dark faces in his city, after five years of all these unspeakable daily hardships, Ben had dared, no, actually been bold enough to contact him.
Instead of five years of city stink, daily stink, gray everyday life, he could have spent five years in the sun of life. And now Ben, who owed him everything, his greatest enemy, had dared

to write to him, to invite him to spend two weeks at the finca.

Why had he actually accepted? Of course he had. In five years, he had done a lot of research on Ben and tracked down a whole series of gray spots in his past. He would go there, play the old friend for a few days and then, over a meal with the old lady who still remembered him, yes, he would tell the old lady the truth. He bit his lips. An eye for an eye, a tooth for a tooth.

The three of them were sitting on the spacious terrace. The property stood on the hill of a small bay, with a comfortable view of the sea from three sides. From the end of the garden, hundreds of steps led down to the snow-white beach. It had become chilly. The old lady suggested going inside.

Ben had already lit the open fire, the natural stones returning the stored cozy warmth to the room. He reached into his jacket pocket again. Ben's gray stains were in this envelope. He didn't really expect the old lady to hire him afterwards.

Maybe she would, he could act as her savior from this criminal Ben. He would wait and see how everything developed. For now, it was enough for

him if Ben was dismissed. The other thing would be a nice bonus.
The three of them sat by the fire. His hand slipped into his jacket pocket and pulled out the envelope. Ben suspected nothing. The old woman was a little surprised at his behavior, the letter he had taken out. He looked at Ben again. Five unnecessary, stuffy office years came back to him. How many firesides had he missed? How many trips to Switzerland? How many, how many, how many. He tore open the envelope, Ben looked at him, startled, intuitively startled, perhaps. The fire crackled, the old lady's eyes flickered in the glow of the flames.

I wanted, he began, I wanted to tell you how pleased I was about your invitation. Yes, I was really pleased. It is a highlight of the last five years of my life.
Then he took the envelope and threw it into the flames.

Sorry, a trivial letter, I've been carrying it around with me for a long time. Just makes a bulge in my jacket.
He got up and left the room without saying a word.

If anyone slaps you on the right cheek, turn to them the other cheek also.
But I tell you, love your enemies and pray for those who persecute you, that you may be children of your Father in heaven. He causes his sun to rise on the evil and the good, and sends rain on the righteous and the unrighteous. (Matthew 5:39,44,45)

Please come back. The old woman's shaky voice was filled with the warmth of the fireplace, the burnt paper having added fuel to the fire. I would like to talk to you about something.
The last words reached his ear when he had already set foot outside the house and penetrated his tiredness of the previous evening like an unreal dream.

5.
The Greatest Small One

Is it cancer?

Yes.

I thought so. How long, how long will I live? The doctor was silent.

Is it months or years?

We are a science. Medicine is an empirical science. I can't tell you. Experience will tell. She was now 43 years old. Two of the three children already in puberty, a house, only a small part paid off, her husband in a difficult professional situation.

What do you suggest?

I can't suggest anything to you.
The doctor's voice faltered. He had known the woman for many years. Why had she come so late? All the suggestions were nothing more than an ordeal, the result at best a few months longer life. But at what cost.

I'll be honest with you. Medicine has struggled with this for a long time, with itself, with the truth, with openness. My gut feeling is that it's best to be open with you. You have a family. There are things to sort out. At 43, hardly anyone has thought about what things there are to sort out.

She sobbed. Every word penetrated her, deeply, not hurtfully, but it was the truth, and truth can be very painful.

Your children need to be prepared for this, the doctor continued.

Your two eldest will, forgive me for putting it this way, they will get over it quickly. The problems of puberty will distract them.

She nodded.

In two or three years, they'll wake up, wake up from a dream as if nothing had happened, realize that I'm no longer with them. Is that what you mean?

Yes, life has built-in protection mechanisms. Puberty is like a protection for your eldest not to be broken by their fate. I don't know, your youngest daughter, will she be able to cope?

The doctor knew that he was conveying fear with these words. Instead of offering comfort. But this fear was real, well-founded and did not cease to exist just because it was hushed up.

Thank you for your frankness. This night is going to be bad. Can you prescribe something to help me sleep?

The doctor went to the medicine cabinet and got a sedative.

I would like to ask you to take a seat in the waiting room for a few more minutes.

She rose without a word. After an hour, the last patients had been treated and the receptionist had left the surgery 15 minutes earlier, the door opened. The doctor stood in front of her, no longer in his white coat, his briefcase tucked under his arm.

Sometimes you don't know what's right. You'll think I'm odd, maybe crazy. You should talk to your children tomorrow. The sooner the better. Your youngest daughter, how old is she?

Eight years old, why do you ask?

I would like to give you something. For your youngest. Just for her. Promise me you won't read it? And don't tell your daughter where you got it. Just put it in her hand and explain to her that it's a secret, just for her.

The doctor remained silent. What he was doing was irresponsible. To place this burden on an eight-year-old girl. It was nothing more than an unauthorized experiment. If it failed, and it would fail, how could he bear the child's disappointment? But he had no other advice. These thoughts had come to him from somewhere.

He handed the woman an envelope.

Give this letter to your daughter. After you have told her everything. When you are both alone. It's from an old book. I think it will help your daughter. Perhaps.

The hustle and bustle of the surgery was over. She was sitting again in front of the doctor, who was studying the X-ray findings over the rim of his glasses.

I'm not a radiologist, the doctor said, I have to rely on the findings. The CT scan showed nothing.

His voice was cool, matter-of-fact, only those who knew him well noticed a slight vibration in his tones. She stared at him in disbelief.

A year ago, I was a hopeless case for you.

Not for me. For the medical profession. For empiricism. There are misdiagnoses. Admittedly. But such a finding could not have been a misdiagnosis. The findings had not been mixed up.

She remained silent because she sensed that other thoughts were running through the doctor's head.

Self-healing is known. A few cases. At least some have been described. Have you changed your life?

A lot, she replied, in a situation like this you change a lot.

You must have a strong will, the doctor continued. There are people with an irrepressible will to live. You must be one of them.

I wanted to ask you something. Back then, a year ago. You gave me something for my youngest daughter. I have the feeling that I shouldn't ask her myself. What did you write back then?

The doctor shook his head.

I don't understand it myself. The words were suddenly there, at some point I had read them in an old book. It wouldn't do you any good if I told you. Even if your daughter told you. At some moment in your life you come to a point where it suddenly pops into your head. I think it will, anyway.

He stood up and shook her hand.

Try to see life with different eyes. The scent of flowers, the chirping of birds, the waves of the sea, a mosquito in the evening light and – your daughter. She will soon be three or four years older. Enjoy it while she is still so small. It will never come back.

Whoever humbles himself as this child is the greatest in the kingdom of heaven.
(Matthew 18:4)

If anyone says to this mountain, 'Go, throw yourself into the sea,' and does not doubt in their heart but believes that what they say will happen, it will be done for them.
(Mark 11:23)

6.
Frozen Donation

They had both set aside €700. This could be used for a few pleasant things, a short trip, a year of regular visits to the theater followed by a meal, a wardrobe update, a new picture for the living room, the long-awaited TV chair.

Television. There was the solution.

We want to do something permanent with it. Something we can enjoy for a long time. Something that will still be there when we're gone, said the man.

What are you thinking of? she asked.

Well, there are a few possibilities. Donate ten new park benches. Each one has a golden sign on it: donated by Hans and Hannelore Bauschhaar.

People will come by, she replied. Young couples in love. To sit down. Enjoying their love. Perhaps remembering that a Hans and a Hannelore were once so young and in love.

He protested: What do you mean were? Young, certainly, but in love? You know I love you like the first day.

Yes, she sighed, hearing the hollow sound in his words.

Take on a sponsorship at the zoo, he continued. The zoo has no money. How about a sponsorship. Sometimes it gets in the papers.

Do you really think so?

Yes, in the local section. I read about it last week, even the names of the donors were listed.

Everyone will read our names, she sighed. Even the tenants in our building. They'll think: The Bauschhaars, they're honorable people. They could have knocked the money on the head. And what do they do with it? Donate it to something sensible so that everyone can enjoy it.

I'm not sure if it gets in the paper every time though. Maybe last week was just some kind of advertisement to get more people to donate.

Bread for the needy, she sighed. Have you seen the poster opposite?

He shook his head and stood up. There was a new poster on the other side of the street. Only one child was depicted, his eyes staring into space. Below it was a notice: For two euros a month, you can give this child an education. Our future belongs to children.

Three children, he quickly calculated, it could provide a life for three children for 20 years. And what for? So that they die in the next civil war, the next famine, the next epidemic, so that they die of AIDS or in the civil war.

You're right, she sighed.

Financially speaking, not a safe investment. The park benches would last at least 50 years or a cage in the zoo, thousands of people could enjoy it for 50 years.

She opened a newspaper.

No, she sighed, as much as I can understand your thoughts, they're not good thoughts. We'll donate the money to people. And we'll let everyone know.

What do you mean? Who cares about a bank transfer slip on which I donate €700 to people in the Third World!

No paper, she replied. Why don't you take a look at this ad in the TV magazine? Next Saturday there is a program from Action Care & Child. Every few minutes they show the names of the donors. Just imagine: Parottidi sings and then the TV displays: Hans and Hannelore Bauschhaar, €700. Millions will see it. The others in the house will see it. Our families will see it. Your work colleagues will see it.

That's how it was decided. Five days later, they were both sitting in front of the television. There was a large plate of sandwiches in front of them, he had placed a cold beer next to it, she a hot tea.

Have you turned on the tape recorder? she wanted to know.

Yes, he nodded. I'll run the other one in the bedroom just to be on the safe side.

You always think of everything, she sighed. I've called my sister. Marga's recording the show too.

Satisfied, he bit into the sandwich and washed the gray lump down into his full stomach with a swig from the beer bottle. The program rippled along. A title bar displayed the names with the amount of the donation. Their names weren't there, not yet.

We're doing very well with €700, he realized. Most people have only donated €100 or a little more, the others are companies. We can't keep up with them.

If they don't show our names, she sighed, it will all be for nothing.

I don't even want to think about such an injustice, he replied. Even if it was embarrassing, why shouldn't we ask for our donation back? There has to be order. We could go over the park benches...

Hey, look! she shouted frantically.

The star tenor was singing on the television and a new streaming bar appeared. There was obviously a technical problem. The streaming bar, which moved continuously from right to left, suddenly stood still and their names appeared on the TV for at least two minutes: Hans and Hannelore Bauschhaar, €700. He was also beside himself.

Do you know how much a minute of advertising costs? His eyes glanced at the clock. They've been advertising for us in front of 15 million people for two minutes. It would have cost us a fortune. Not even the biggest car brand has such a long commercial.

The phone rang. They both jumped up at the same time. But he let her go first. She just kept quiet during the call, her eyes wide open, her mouth even wider.

Who was it? he asked when she had hung up the phone.

Marga. She was completely beside herself. She couldn't believe it.

Her words had barely died away when the phone rang again. To be fair, this time it was his turn.

You won't believe it, he blurted out at the end of the call. Guess who called me?

My mother? she asked.

He shook his head.

Someone from the family?

His head shaking became more violent.

Someone from work?

Yes, but who?

Not your boss?

Believe it or not. It was my boss. Congratulations, he said, we need people with social commitment.

Unbelievable, she sighed.

What a return, he whispered. It's not 10%, it's not 20%, it can't be expressed as a percentage at all.

She squeezed his hand. Her pride went right to the tips of her fingers. He silently enjoyed it and looked at the television.

At least 20, he thought, and his mind was already at work the next morning.

Yes, she sighed, sensing his thoughts through their clasped hands, and I think there will be more colleagues who saw it.

Mm, he mumbled, maybe you're right. But I'll tell you all about it when I get home in the evening. So it might be a bit later. Maybe everyone will insist on a round of beer in the pub opposite to celebrate

Fine, she sighed, while the pressure in her hand grew like a mustard seed with the pride in her heart.

So when you give to the needy, do not announce it with trumpets, as the hypocrites do in the synagogues and on the streets, to be honored by others. (Matthew 6:2)

7.
Rocky Sand

Every year, every year they went to the seaside. Brittany, rocks, scenery, coast. The two children didn't protest, they were only six and seven years old, why should they, why disco, city stroll, pub crawl, here on the beach there was everything, stones, sand, strange animals, shells, sea urchins, fossils thousands of years old, seaweed woven into bizarre shapes, huge rocks from another world, everything was here, much more than in reality.

We're going to build a castle, said Janine.
She was six years old, brunette hair, a miniature mirror of her mother. Both parents were lying under the parasol, asleep.

No, the boy refused.
Pascal was the older of the two, a boy and a year older, there were two crucial differences, at least at this stage of life.

Everyone builds for themselves. You back there. I'll build here by mom and dad.

Janine thought about it. For a moment she thought about protesting, but immediately realized the futility of this endeavor and ran down the beach. She stopped after 30 meters. Her brother was no longer looking at her. He was already digging in the sand with his spade and heaping up huge mountains. Everything was more difficult for her.
Large round stones lay on top of each other, rocks, in between flat pieces of gray sea sand, old shells glowed between the rocks in the bright sunlight, the damp underside of the dried seaweed exuded an unpleasant smell, swarms of flies shot into the air when she picked up a shell. She chose a flat rock-like stone and began to heap up sand. She fortified the walls with driftwood, washed between the rocks by the waves. Her castle was not high, but the outer walls were decorated with hundreds of different kinds of limestone animals.

I used to believe in justice.
The two men sat in the street café, their eyes gliding over the waves.

Justice, replied the other. Justice is always determined by others. Then you've done nothing but believe in others. What a stupid thing to do.

No, the first one disagreed vehemently. There must be something independent. Something that is independent of me and you and all 10 billion people.

Even of your boss? You've seen what's independent of him. You've been fired. Where is the justice? Where is this something that is independent of everyone, including your boss?

Maybe you're right. I always thought, it won't happen to you. You worked diligently for seven years, always did a little more than expected, sometimes dragged yourself to work sick. It was all swept away.

The two men looked down at the open sea again. Down on the beach, the two children were playing. The wind drove countless, rising waves onto the land and the tide slowly began to rise.

Swept away, said one of them. That's exactly the right word. You feel safe, it won't hit you, no storm will knock you down – and now this.

You have to look at it more neutrally, replied the other. You've been hit, that's true. But you haven't fallen over yet. Even if you might feel that way, but they're two different shoes, the blow is one thing, falling over is another.

It's all very well for you to talk. Your life is going smoothly.

If only you knew, thought the person he was talking to, if only you knew. We all get knocks from life, from fate, from friends, from strangers, from enemies, from all possible sides.

Janine, Pascal, it's time! The woman's shrill voice cut through the air. Her eyes, awakened from the dream, gathered the children.

The boy pulled his father up. By the time he was standing, the girl had arrived.

You have to see my castle, Pascal shouted and pulled his father away.

In the last hour, he had heaped up an imposing structure that lived up to its Norman origins. The father was visibly proud, but avoided an overly exuberant reaction because of the girl.

Do you want to see my castle? asked Janine.

We're going for an ice cream, replied her mother, we have to go to the right, then we'll pass your castle.

Janine nodded and ran ahead. After a few moments, her parents arrived with her brother.

Lovely, Janine, said the father. And what beautiful shell walls. And now, now we're looking forward to a huge ice cream that's colder than the North Pole.

The children ran ahead, up the dunes, slowly followed by their parents.

How different the two are, said the father. I think our boy will grow up to be something big. Did you see what he had built in such a short time?

Yes, his wife replied. Maybe you can continue building together later. I think Pascal would be thrilled.

While they sat at the ice cream parlor and everyone cooled off with a large portion, the wind and tide drove the water into the bay. There was also shopping to be done.

It was evening, until they had time before the night shore, time to walk down to the beach once more. The girl's castle sparkled in the glowing red of the setting sun. It stood like a fiery house on the rock, at the foot of which lay newly washed up driftwood.

Otherwise the beach was empty, everything washed away.

Therefore everyone who hears these words of mine and puts them into practice is like a wise man who built his house on the rock. The rain came down, the streams rose, and the winds blew and beat against that house; yet it did not fall, because it had its foundation on the rock.
(Matthew 7:24,25).

The two men stood up. They had been sitting in the beach café all afternoon. Their legs had become heavy.

You're right, said the first one.

He was glad to be able to stand up again after such a long time and stretch his limbs.

We all get knocked about. But I'm not going to get knocked down.

He looked down, looked at his feet resting on the smooth old rocks of Brittany's beach.

8.
The Insider

It was undoubtedly the most important game of the year, the most important game in his coaching career. And this had already lasted ten years. He was finally on the verge. Just before the championship. After more than 30 games, just one last step and then – the other clubs would be all over him; a triumphal procession in the motorcade through the city lined with people, a reception with the mayor, his name in the city's golden book, the view from the town hall over the tens of thousands, his wife's proud, silent look at the success, all the doors would open imperceptibly for the children, in school, training, career.

Just one more game. But it had to be won.

One week's time.

In front of him lay the sheet with the names of all the players. He had made entries throughout the season. The number one, the goalkeeper, was set. He was half the battle. If he was on form, success was already assured. He hadn't conceded a goal in the last few games. And since he had a striker, number nine, who had scored a goal in every game so far, the result was already certain. At least one-nil, no goals conceded, that was the zero, at least one goal scored by number nine, that was the one.

He didn't have to change the back four. It was the best defensive unit in the league. And, two of them had not yet won a title, they were eager for this game to become champions themselves. There will be a zero at the back, he summed it up by saying that his best defense was playing against the worst strikers. The opposition had scored fewer goals than any other team. Not even one goal per game.

Number one and the back four, he repeated, writing the players' names on a sheet. I'm not going to change that.

But now came the point where his decision was not clear. Which system should he play? 4-4-2 or 4-3-3? He was a gut man, at least when it came to important decisions. He immediately had a sure feeling about 4-4-2. It would be the right playing system. Two defensive midfielders in front of the defense, number eight and number 20, with his two aggressive attacking

midfielders in front of them, both of whom were also capable of scoring goals.
Number nine was set in the forward line, he was good for a goal in every game. Only the second striker remained open. The longer he thought about it, the less he could decide. Even his instincts let him down. Everything remained open. The days passed, the training sessions, he couldn't make up his mind.

It was the last afternoon before the game. In his head, his team was set. Except for the second striker. It didn't matter at first. He had scheduled a 20-minute talk with each player for the afternoon. He wanted to brief each player individually on the game, introduce them to the tactics and make them realize the importance of this match one last time.
The assistant coach led the training sessions on the pitch. He had a bench set up on the sidelines where he held the conversations. He wanted the team to feel his presence, his authority, he didn't want to disappear somewhere into a dressing room or a remote club office in these final hours.

After the second meeting, he had the feeling that he was doing something superfluous. The players were motivated down to their toenails. There was no need to talk. On the contrary, there was a danger of over-motivation. They had discussed the tactics hundreds of times, the motivation was perfect, he had to be careful not to over-motivate the team. Nevertheless, he sensed that the icing on the cake was missing, something unusual that neither the team nor their opponents were expecting.
Of course, it flashed through his mind. I'm going to play. Not tomorrow in the championship game. Today, at the last training match. They only know me in a suit and tie or from the sidelines.
They were all more than stunned when their coach suddenly stood among them in shorts. His movements revealed that he had once been good on the ball, but his age, the fat deposits and the lack of smoothness in his movements could not be overlooked. It did not detract. Everyone was delighted, he and the team, it was the icing on the cake that had been missing.
The players saw him as their equal and like a father who looked after them without standing aloof above them. They hadn't had this special

atmosphere in recent years. It was a sudden flash of inspiration, his feeling, that gave him this brilliant idea.

The training match had been going on for half an hour. A sharp ball came into the penalty area from the far right. All he had to do was head it in, intuitively as before. The ball smashed from his head to the bottom of the crossbar and from there into the goal. Before he knew it, a crowd of players had formed around him. He, the coach, had been the first to get past number one, their star goalkeeper. What a goal! Wimbledon was nothing compared to that.

Go on, go on! he shouted, pushing up the players lying on top of him.

Both training teams ran into their half to line up for the kick-off. He trotted along the touchline, his place was at the back of midfield. As he passed the substitutes' bench, his eyes fell on Kalle. Unpleasant feelings welled up inside him. Sure, this Kalle was one of the most talented strikers, but he made nothing of it. Last week, he had had to suspend him from training when he turned up drunk. Indiscipline, womanizing and now drinking, plus a pack of cigarettes a day. The team had distanced itself from Kalle. After the season, Kalle was available for transfer and the club would let him go. That was the end of the problem for him.

For a tiny moment, his eyes fell into Kalle's stare. Suddenly his feeling, his sense of an impending decision, overcame him. When he left the pitch, the team was hugely disappointed.

What's wrong, coach?

No more enthusiasm?

Where is your commitment?

He felt the great psychological misfortune of his decision. For the first time, the team had the feeling that he was one of them, that he really cared about them because it was important to him, not just because he was the coach. And at that moment, he left the team. He couldn't have done anything worse before the important game. But there was this Kalle, there was his feeling that left him no other choice. While he was still discussing things with the team, Kalle had disappeared into the dressing room. He ran after him and sat down next to the player without saying a word.

What do you want, coach? Kalle asked.

To talk.

Don't bother. You said yourself that I'm no longer part of the team.

That's true. You know why.

Yes, you were right. But you could have done it differently without embarrassing me in front of the team.

You've put yourself on the sidelines.

Yes, Kalle replied. If someone has fallen into the pit, they don't need anyone else to step on them.

But now you're twisting things around. His voice became angry.

Let's leave that alone. Tomorrow the season is over. And my time in the team.

Both were silent. Suddenly the door opened. Two players appeared.

You have to come, said number nine to the coach. The team insists on finishing the training game with you.

He looked at the two players. They were his two most important ones. The goalkeeper and number nine, always good for a goal, always good against a goal.

I'm honored, he replied. Unfortunately, I can't. Take the assistant coach in my place.

Their disappointment was palpable, like a meter thick cold wall. They left the room in silence.

You'll play tomorrow, he said to Kalle. Second striker next to number nine.

Kalle remained silent. Then he suddenly said:

No. You've kicked me out. Go and join the team. It's better that way.

Listen Kalle, the contract runs until the end of the season. You'll play tomorrow. I'm going to put your name last on the players' sheet.

The next day, the atmosphere in the team crackled like dry gunpowder. Nobody understood the coach's decision.

The first half was a total disaster. The score stood at zero but twice it was only the post that saved them, and nothing was going right in midfield or up front. Nevertheless, he made no changes to the line-up. The minutes ticked by. In the 75th minute, their right-back broke through for the first time and delivered a sharp ball into the middle. Number nine soared high but was pulled over by an opposing defender grabbing his jersey. The penalty whistle came immediately.

They all looked at each other. Number nine ran to the ball and placed it on the penalty spot.

As a coach, he had no other choice. He jumped up angrily. In his day, it was a firm law that the fouled player was not allowed to take the penalty.

You don't shoot, Gerd, he shouted to his number nine.

Everyone was confused. Number nine angrily left the penalty area. Nobody dared to step forward. The referee looked impatiently at his watch. Number 22, Kalle, came forward from behind. He silently walked past the others and corrected the position of the ball.

What do you think? If a man owns a hundred sheep, and one of them wanders away, will he not leave the ninety-nine on the hills and go to look for the one that wandered off? And if he finds it, truly I tell you, he is happier about that one sheep than about the ninety-nine that did not wander off. (Matthew 18:12,13)

A week later, he was standing on the town hall balcony as a coach. His name was inscribed in the town's golden book. They had driven through the city in an open motorcade. His thoughts went back. He had known that the penalty kick would be the only real chance of scoring. He looked down. People were standing around everywhere, in groups of ninety-nine, the square was full of them. Every now and then he recognized two forlorn eyes, forlorn eyes in the middle of the endless crowd.

9.
Power of Abuse of Power

Mr. Justthere had worked his way up, in the truest sense of the word. He had been born in the lowest part of the city, where something like slum formation had begun. And that was not all. His family lived in a basement apartment, not much light, a lot of damp earthy cold, all you could see of the people were mostly their legs, fast and leisurely, brisk, restrained, all kinds of steps, but only their legs. The soles of the shoes were also interesting, at least for a child, with all the things stuck to them, crushed leaves, dead beetles, nails, splinters of wood, dog excrement. So that's what the world looked like from below, dark, a many-shaded gray, but always just gray.

But life made up for it, if only someone wanted it to. Anyone could work their way up from the dirt – and he had done it – high school diploma without school fees, studies thanks to scholarships, a career as a senior civil servant, early entry into the ruling party, first deputy

local chairman, now its leader and, in addition, mayor of the city for four years.
His office was on the top floor of the town hall, perched on a small hill in the middle of the city, overlooking everything. He no longer saw the soles of life, crushed leaves, dead beetles, trampled nails and splinters of wood, dried animal droppings. He looked at people's most sensitive spots. On her head, he saw round bald patches – vainly concealed, garishly tinted strands of hair, children's curls amidst butterfly barrettes, the dyed gray hair of vain women – and men.
Up here, nobody looked at his head.
Now he was the boss. The past was behind him, forgotten, finished, a discarded, cast-off piece of clothing.
It had gotten even better. Everything could always be better. His country, his life, had been built on this philosophy. No-one saw the dead end at the end of the supposed ladder to heaven.
For a year now, he had been living, no, residing in an old manor house, in the upper part of the city, also on a small hill, lapped by the gentle bends of the river that meandered through the conglomerate of people. The years had made him

confident, very confident. He maintained his marriage to his wife for the sake of the outside world. It was nothing more than a show partnership, the hollow walls leaning shakily against each other, an advantage for both of them, because that way none of the cold hollow walls collapsed.

He had first noticed her a month ago when he paid a visit to the head of the building department. She was perhaps thirty years old, naturally blonde and blue-eyed, long legs up to her neck, raised by heels, barely a third covered by a short skirt, long red fingernails that scratched across the paper as she wrote. The rest was routine. He created a new post to intensify relations with the twin cities. His exploratory speculations proved him right. She also applied for this position, alongside twenty other candidates, all of them more highly qualified.

I don't need a theoretician, I need a practitioner, he had said in the meeting. Ms. Sopretty is exactly the right person. We have five twin towns. She has lived in three of them for several years. I don't need a shyster, but someone with experience.

Of course, he had studied her CV beforehand and therefore decided on a position to intensify partner relations. If necessary, he would have created a position to assess cosmetics in terms of new urban trends if her only qualification had been the utilization of a particularly large number of these products.

And he soon let her know to whom she owed this position. Again, he had judged her correctly. The new post had doubled her salary, and if he had been even more interested, he would have been able to triple it in a short time.

The first few weeks of their affair justified this investment. In a way, she was the intermediary through which he concubined with the twin towns. Intensifying the twinning relationship with the other towns was worth something to the taxpayer. The flow of visitors between the six towns would increase and tourism would bring in money everywhere.

Everything was fine until this snoot, this Mr. Againstyou, turned up. Not only did he pounce on his prey, he was also the son of his first landlord and he had anything but pleasant memories of him.

One afternoon, he was sitting in the office with his personal press officer.

How long have you been with me now, Mr. Openmouth, he asked.

Two years, Mr. Justthere, for a good two years.

He cleared his throat.

And now, Mr. Openmouth, tell me how long you were unemployed before that.

The other man was embarrassed.

Three years, he croaked, a little less than three years.

Have you heard of anyone in this country who has catapulted from three years of unemployment to become a mayor's press spokesman?

No, Mr. Justthere.

You know how many awkward questions it cost me. And you know why I called you in.

The other one shrugged his shoulders.

You know very well. I can deal with those from the press on my own. I don't need you for that. You're my all-purpose cleaning tool.

Your what? If you don't mind me asking.

You're not allowed to. You see, a certain Mr. Againstyou works in the art department. I'll give

you four weeks, Openmouth, then this guy will have disappeared, not just from the office, but completely from the scene, without civil servant status, preferably as a tramp under a bridge or in prison. Why am I spending so much money on prison buildings?
The press officer gulped. He had no choice. It wasn't just about him, it was about his family, the car, the neighbors' respect, regular family vacations twice a year, new shoes, good food on the table.
He managed it in three and a half weeks. Againstyou had been suspended from office and was under investigation for false expense claims, suspected corruption and misappropriation of funds. The least he could expect was the loss of his civil servant status, perhaps even a suspended sentence with a criminal record.
When he heard the news, he met with her that same evening. The office had been cleaned up, an old debt with his first landlord had been settled, he had worked his way up, worked his way up at work, worked his way down with the woman.
It was a different feeling tonight than before, not uninteresting, very satisfying. When he had finished, he let himself fall contentedly to the

side. She lit a cigarette. Actually, he hated women who smoked, especially those who smoked afterwards. He looked at the body that had become familiar. Ms. Sopretty had become a bad investment. She didn't fill the position in the slightest. Nothing had changed in relations with the twin towns. Soon there would be unrest at the municipal meeting. He could least do with that now. The elections were coming up. But their affair had not yet lasted long, had not yet paid off.

He calculated figures for how often they were together and put it in relation to the tax money invested. At this level, the investment really hadn't paid off yet. He would maintain the affair for another three months and then call his press officer Openmouth in for a meeting. That might mean creating another position.

There was also someone from the family to accommodate. He had actually thought about Ms. Sopretty's new position. He decided against this solution. Many things had to be intensified. An urgently needed area of responsibility would be found somewhere. After all, he was the boss.

You know that the rulers of the Gentiles lord it over them, and their high officials exercise authority over them. Not so with you. Instead, whoever wants to become great among you must be your servant, and whoever wants to be first must be your slave. (Matthew 20:25-27)

10.
Remorseful Penetrance

Can we?

The boy shook his head.

No, he's really angry with us.

Because of yesterday?

Yes, because of yesterday. I knew it right away.

The girl thought about it. Yesterday. Yesterday had passed. Was it fair to make a decision for tomorrow dependent on yesterday?

What do you think, asked the boy.

He watched his silent sister.

That it's your fault. I mean because of yesterday.

Now you're going crazy. We both came home late. You were even later than me, I got into the house before you.

Not exactly gentlemanly!

So what? Is it ladylike to put all the blame on me now?

That's not the point at all. But you wanted to stay. I told you at least three times that we had to go home.

Three times. You've been bugging me about it all evening. Do you know how long I haven't seen Sabine? A year. Exactly one year. And suddenly I bump into her at the party. Even though she was supposed to be at high school in America.

Now they were both silent. She was 17, her brother a year younger. Yesterday they had come home two hours late. The big thunderstorm hadn't materialized. More of a dry thunderstorm. No verbose outpourings, a simple, curt no.

We could ask mother, the boy suggested.

Doesn't work anymore, she replied. I have a feeling they've been colluding lately. To form a front. Clever maneuver.

Is he very angry?

I don't know. He just sits in front of the TV and watches soccer. You get the impression he's not even listening. Waits until you've recited his psalm and just says: No. He didn't even look up.

Then there's probably nothing we can do.

Let's try again. I really want to go to the meeting. I've been looking forward to it for a month.

They both took a deep breath. They left their conspiratorial room and entered the living room. Her father was sitting in the armchair. The sport was still on. They retreated into the hallway.

What should we say? she whispered.

I don't know, the boy replied. It was your idea to try a second time.

Then let's think about it first.

A few minutes passed and the commentator's insistent report sounded from the room. Neither of them could think of anything to say. They waited until the break and then entered the room. Neither of them knew how to try until the end.

Their father looked up.

United general attack? he said dryly. You needn't bother.

We're sorry, said the girl. We could at least have called.

That's probably true. Can you imagine how worried we are if you don't get home on time. There are telephones. There are cell phones. There are text messages. And there's so much that can happen.

That's why we're coming, the boy said. We tried to put ourselves in your shoes. It's certainly not cool as parents to sit at home and not know what's going on with the kids.
He nodded.

Not cool is probably a bit of an understatement.

We have a suggestion, she interjected. We're sorry about yesterday. It was total crap. But we promise it won't happen again. In any case, we'll work hard on it for the next four weeks.
He looked at both of them.

Looks like you must care a lot about tonight. Your promise, do you really mean it?
They both nodded. They both raised their hands and gave their father a handshake one after the other, something they had been doing since childhood to seal something special.
Again, truly I tell you that if two of you on earth agree about anything they ask for, it will be done for them by my Father in heaven.
(Matthew 18:19)
Their hands loosened.

Now get out of here, their father said. 11 p.m., no later.

They grumbled a little, but felt that any further discussion had already been answered.

And don't forget your cell phones.

Outside, she nudged her brother.

Let's really be on time.

He nodded.

You have my word. Today and for the next four weeks and longer.

She nudged him again.

The conversation was cool, she said. At first, I didn't know what I wanted to say.

Yes, he replied, and when you started, I immediately realized what I could do to help. The two of us make a great team.

11.
Too Close Neighbor

Of course it was a convenience. It was just part of the job. As a dignitary, he was entitled to his own house, a domestic help, a personal assistant and a company car with chauffeur. This is where equality began, as far as it was allowed to go. He had hired a female chauffeur. Middle-aged. It made the journeys much more pleasant.

He sat in the back of the spacious limousine. An exhausting meeting lay behind him. The tight financial situation in his area could no longer be ignored. In a few years, they would sell the first church. It was mostly empty anyway. As pioneers, the first congregation had separated off part of the nave, converted it into condominiums and then sold it to a wealthy clientele. There was nothing wrong with this, he never made this decision official, it was within what was tolerable, within the bounds of his generous heart – just like the three million that came into the empty coffers as a result.

Only the windows to the worship room put a damper on his mood. What horror, unbelieving worshippers comfortably seated in soft upholstered armchairs, drinking champagne on Sunday morning, while at the same time taking part in the service through the gap in the windows.

Turn down the next street. I am thinking of resting my head, we don't want to rush our return.

The chauffeur understood his words. She switched off the flashing lights again and the car sped straight ahead, following the well-kept emptiness of the road at a smooth speed.

Turn back, the usual way. My eyes will look, little of the night's doings, unrepentant souls, gone astray.

She nodded again. The awkward instruction meant nothing more than turning right three intersections down the road, where the black of night turned into the red of sin.

She slowed down so that his old eyes could soak up the darkness. The girls of the night stood strung together, sparkling pearls of a string between the lanterns. A summer night rolled through the city, the bodies heated by the glow of the days. Like beacons, the warmth radiated from their scantily clad bodies.

They sin, he said, sin in the blackness of the night, thinking their sins to be hidden by the blackness of the night.

The chauffeur remained silent. It was not the first time that the limousine she was driving had divided the city district. A plow that made cuts in the body of the earth, swelling human suffering and misery on both sides.

I need a stop, he murmured, her ahead at the next corner.

She brought the car to a halt. He manhandled one of the girls to him.

Just talk, his voice quoted the thoughts of the head, make yourself comfortable in the car.

The woman shifted from the lamppost and leaned on the comfortable back seat. His fingers intertwined, making bizarre movements, his senses ogling and sucking in the woman.

If any one of you is without sin, let him be the first to throw a stone at her. (John 8:7)

I am without a stone, he said. Nevertheless, your life is not right. You should do housework, not street work, mother in the house, children, they are a great responsibility.

She remained silent. Good thing he only wanted to talk. Maybe look too, but it didn't hurt.

300, she suddenly blurted out. Words are expensive. I'm going with you for an hour. It will cost you 300.

200, he objected. Souls are expensive, of course. There are many. Let's do business, a big offer, the price is getting lower.

She was tired of negotiating. When he squeezed the two bills into her hand, she felt his cool skin for a second. Cold as stone. He was without stones. Maybe she couldn't see into every corner of his existence after all. Without stones, she thought, his whole hand is a stone.

Insights are the beginning, he continued. A tower in the storm of life. From there, life jumps back onto the path most easily.

What did he know? She had insights every night, into every conceivable shade of that which called itself human.

You shall love your neighbor as yourself. (Matthew 22:39)

You'll be with me next, he murmured. Loving means forgiving. A commandment. Loving means commanding.

Her body shook. The existence of the feelings was inexplicable. They came, often without consideration, appearing out of nowhere.
Suddenly the car stopped. The chauffeur had spotted a crowd of people. They were circling a collapsed human figure that had fallen to the cold ground.

Our way continues, he called forward.
They stripped him of his clothes, beat him and went away, leaving him half dead. A priest happened to be going down the same road, and when he saw the man, he passed by on the other side. (Luke 10:30-31)

Keep driving, he commanded. It must always go on. Everything flows. Death to stagnation.
He turned up the collar of his jacket, his face disappearing from the crowd behind the dark fabric. Her foot pressed on the car's accelerator. Slowly, the heavy metal vehicle began to move. The woman wrenched open the car door and rushed outside. With sweeping movements, she dispersed the crowd and knelt in front of the crashed human satellite body. As the ride slowly picked up speed, he took one last look at her exposed, kneeling legs.

We're going to do a house sweep, he ordered his chauffeur.
She understood and steered the car back the direct way.
Truly I tell you, the tax collectors and the prostitutes are entering the kingdom of God ahead of you. (Matthew 21:31)
He reached to the side. He had long since noticed that the woman had deliberately left the two banknotes behind.

I need air to breathe, he said, and his chauffeur flicked a lever so that his side window opened. He stuck his hand out and threw the two banknotes out. Never in his life would he put them in the offering box, because the sullied eyes of love stuck to them.

12.
Wrestle With Death

Toot, toot, tooot, toooot, tooooooooooo...
Gone. The line shown had become a horizontal line, a zero line. The old woman had made it. She had been admitted an hour earlier. Intestinal bleeding, gallons of it, her face as white as a sheet. The doctor on duty had inserted a central IV, quite a feat given her circulatory conditions. Now the small, gray body lay on the hospital bed, its temperature slowly cooling, its movements frozen in death.
What does someone feel when they die? What do the others feel when someone dies? It was the time when the first reports, the first books, appeared with experiences from this borderline area. We read about accident victims who saw their bodies floating in the air, surrounded by onlookers and helpers.
Of the clinically dead, heart attack, gone, over, in a second, who were torn into a tunnel of light and at the end saw a warm light that made their body glow, recognized a white figure, looking at

them with infinite love, so that they no longer wanted to return to this grey globe.
Only reports, no proof, perhaps feverish fantasies, delirious changes of consciousness in the brain between wakefulness and coma, nothing more than various chemical processes that produced virtual dream images.
Intern, he was just a simple intern, he was just a simple intern back then. When death came, hecticness broke out, orderly hecticness – first a brief dispute as to whether it made sense to resuscitate the old woman. A brief exchange of words, no decision, but as the first white-coated body moved towards the body of the dead woman, an unstoppable automatism took place. He crept into a corner of the room, watching what was happening, really just to get to know death. What would it feel like, what would be felt, what would perhaps be seen when death conquered the white coats. That was all that mattered to him.
To see death for the first time in his life. Before his eyes, he saw the spirit of the old woman hovering under the ceiling, looking helplessly at the goings-on below her, constantly swaying between the ceiling and the sickbed. Mirages,

nothing more than mirages, generated by the death reports he had read a few weeks ago. A few days earlier, he had interviewed a patient who had been successfully resuscitated after a heart attack and clinical death. What had he experienced? The tunnel of light? A tunnel? The warm feeling? The figure of light? Happiness, fear of having to return?

Nothing, it was nothing special that the dead man remembered. Even the first encounter with death, the dying of the old woman, nothing other than someone turning off a switch.

Everything was over. Nothing more.

Why don't you let him die?

Seven years had passed. On the operating table lay the massive body of a man, 1.90 m of body, vessels, nerves, muscles, fat, countless injuries, bleeding from several more places, circulatory shock, impaired blood clotting, the blood clotting had collapsed, blood was creeping to the surface even from uninjured areas.

Let him die. Even if he survives, he has nothing left to live for.

The surgeon looked at his colleague on duty. He was not to be convinced. Death was an enemy. Dying was a lost battle.

We will operate. We'll stop the major bleeding. Then the other one will stop too.
He stuffed meters of gauze into the injured soft tissue, refusing to let the red blood juice escape to the surface. It flowed all the more violently. A large incision divided the abdominal wall, beneath it a lake of blood. Hand by hand, he spooned it into a bowl.
The other man turned away.
Why doesn't he let him die?
Shaking his head.
Seven years had passed, the second time he met death. The battle was bloodier than the first time. The man was just 30 years old, a motorcyclist, rear-end collision, thrown from his motorcycle, his abdomen lying on the trailer coupling of a car.
It was spring outside. The warm sun was shining down dark thoughts of winter. Lovers were sitting in the park. Small children were playing with their parents. Old people dared to leave their homes after months. Plants broke through the earth, green dripped from the branches. The man had got his motorcycle to enjoy the awakening freedom, to glide through the city and through nature, to feel the warm wind, to wave

to other motorcyclists, to press on the accelerator, to rush past lumbering cars.
The man was in the midst of life. Life lay before him. A wide, endless road on which he was gliding. Freedom, sun, warmth, a gentle breeze, the scent of flowers, fresh greenery, the sound of birds, a well-paid job, a nice apartment, a great motorcycle, a day off. It was the life he was living until the moment he crashed into the car, from nothing to nothing.
He thought of the reports again. Souls floating under the ceiling. Light tunnels, at the end the figure of light to receive the newcomer with open arms.
You too, be ready! For the Son of Man is coming at an hour you do not expect. (Matthew 24:44)

No more point, said the surgeon on duty.
He was no longer stuffing gauze into the torn open holes in the body. Over the sterile drapes, his eyes gave the anesthesiologist a brief signal.

His destination was somewhere else, he said, and looked at the table one last time.
Slowly, the curve of the monitor leveled off into a flat straight line, starting at the left of the screen, swept away by the stream of electrons into the infinity of the wire.

13.
Miscalculation

To whom was he beholden? To his colleagues on the board? To the employees? To the shareholders? To his family? To reporters who asked critical questions?
He drew a thick line across the paper. That was it. To no-one, he was beholden to no-one. Not even to his conscience. He was doing a good job, a damn good job, as the balance sheets showed. Admittedly, not always, but there were tricks, tricks were nothing more than floating particles in the lawless space between right and wrong. Every creative economy needed this space. Where was optimism supposed to come from? From confining laws? Stifling paragraphs? Small-minded civil servants in stuffy offices, bearing no responsibility, no risk?
His profit was calculated from the loss. Others lost their jobs, personnel costs went down, profits went up, balance sheets shone, his performance-related salary rose. It rose, rose and rose again, for the seventh year in a row. No

economic downturn could stop it. Broken families? How many were there behind the redundancy figures? Suicides? How many were behind the redundancy figures? Reactive depressions? How many were there behind the redundancy figures? Children affected, young people affected? How many were there behind the redundancy figures?

Don't worry, he reassured himself. You have to lay off a thousand to give 10,000 a place to live. That was the end of the matter.

With the basic salary, the share options and other profit-sharing schemes gave him an annual income of several million. The harvest was good. The field had to be tilled.

What should I do? I don't know where to put my money harvest? he asked himself.

He would build a new house, twice as big as the old one. Plus a farm on the outskirts of the city, for the weekends, also to be self-sufficient, to provide for himself. His own vegetables and meat, why from the discount store, there were reports in the press every day, even scandals in the expensive stores.

He didn't have to endure it. He would be able to watch his Christmas goose for a year beforehand, the smell of the vegetables would waft under his nose for weeks before they made it to the table.

The car was already a year old. Why didn't he have the latest model? We needed two more cars. One for the weekend, one for when he visited family members. The new house was to have a five-car garage, his wife's SUV had to be accommodated, his motorcycle, he hated that his old garage had so little space; every time he had to squeeze the motorcycle between the cars.

He thought about the age of his yacht. Many memories were attached to the boat. Gone. Fresh memories would cling to a new boat like water snails to a boat's keel. The locks had been enlarged in recent years. The new boat could be bigger, indeed he would be able to cover the distance to the open sea with a much larger boat.

He began to write down all these important plans on a piece of paper. His life mind mapping. Underneath, he sketched his own ideas for the boat and the house, wrote the possible car models next to them and...

Sometimes he felt a twinge. Not much. Slightly. A brief tug, not really a twinge. Not even for a second. After that, everything was fine again, in the green zone. He was a little overworked, the stress at work, all the planning, in his private life. He had forgotten about a cruise. Where to, the North Cape or the Mediterranean, the Greek Aegean, the Caribbean, South Africa?

Just a little tug, reminiscent of a twinge, a needle in a haystack of contentment, a little radiation into the arm with which he had gathered all the wealth.

He had achieved more in a short time than many people do in their entire lives. Now it was time to reap the harvest. Settle down, secure the rest of his life with sensible investments, build a decent, large house, and from there conquer the world by traveling.

This time it was knife-like. A stab that went from the spine to the front. The old problem. He had to take it into account by going to the spa for four weeks, crusting his body with healing mud and having all his muscles kneaded by smart physiotherapists. The right preparation before he would enjoy the second half of his life.

Tomorrow he had an appointment with the architect. He had drawn up a few designs himself, an old Prussian tradition; the king had also designed his palace before the master builder turned it into Sanssouci. His Sanssouci was now already on paper. The interior was no less elegant than a royal palace, marble, golden taps, it was the least of it, thick Persian carpets, a fireplace built with granite stones from the Rocky Mountains, the entire wall of the fireplace framed with amber. Here the expenses began to get a little painful, but for him there were too many wealthy people, he had to set himself apart from the common rich.

The phone rang. The car factory. The car he had ordered was handmade from start to finish.

Mr. Hendrik, this is Mr. Smith. I have an inquiry about your order.

He thought about it. After all, everything was fixed.

What's the problem, he said pointedly.

The leather, Mr. Hendrik. As we discussed, we can take it from cattle that have spent their lives in the Scottish Highlands. I just wanted to let you know that there's something better. Moose leather from Finland. Not everyone has it, Mr. Hendrik. Very supple. Exudes a certain cool elegance. And Mr. Hendrik, the animals are specially killed to order. Carefully, because of

the leather. What's more, you can choose whether it's from a cow moose or a bull.
He was taken aback, the salesman noticed immediately.

There are customers, Mr. Hendrik, who care whether they are sitting on something female or something male. Excuse me, I mean in the car. We didn't want to miss the opportunity to point this out to you.

Then take moose, he replied curtly. A moose cow for the driver's seat and a moose bull for the passenger seat. I hope you won't bother me again.
Mr. Smith, the salesman gulped.

My sincere apologies, Mr. Hendrik, and best wishes to your wife.
Actually, the stabbing started in different places. At the back, radiating from the spine to the front, now it shot from the upper abdomen into the chest, stabbed between two ribs and left his body through the outer two fingers of his left hand. Another volley followed.
Now a stabbing pain from the left joined the attack, cold sweat ran down his forehead, the handmade heart motor began to stutter.

Filled with fear, he tried to get up and reach the phone. A violent avalanche of pain knocked him down and he fell to the floor like a plank. His lungs tried to mix the blue blood with air, but his larynx was constricted.

His heart was fibrillating, 300 senseless, uncoordinated muscle twitches a minute. The blood backed up in the lungs, spilled over into the tissue vesicles, foam appeared in his mouth, first whitish, then mixed with traces of red.

The ground of a certain rich man yielded an abundant harvest. He thought to himself, What shall I do? I have no place to store my crops.

Then he said, This is what I'll do. I will tear down my barns and build bigger ones, and there I will store my surplus grain. And I'll say to myself, You have plenty of grain laid up for many years. Take life easy; eat, drink and be merry.

But God said to him, You fool! This very night your life will be demanded from you. Then who will get what you have prepared for yourself? (Luke 12:16-20)

14.
The Cross We Each Have To Bear

There is nothing to be said against the qualifications, absolutely nothing. Or do you see it differently?

No, not really. It's just the gap in his career path that's problematic. Didn't you notice it?

I don't know what you're talking about.

Too many applications. I can understand that. It's impossible to pay attention to every little thing. There's a gap of three years where he obviously didn't work.

Well, that sheds a different light on the application.

Have you seen the photo?

The other man was silent. For a long while. He only replied curtly:

Write to him. Next week Tuesday, 10:30 a.m. in my office. I'll see for myself. And Mr. Google-rt, I would like you to be present at the interview.

Yes sir, do you want me to prepare something? I mean any tests.

Yes, think of something. Have him take the tests like everyone else. Maybe pick some harder ones. A counterweight, if he can't explain three years of his professional career, he must be able to throw a decent counterweight into the balance.

The assistant, Mr. Google-rt, left the HR manager's room. He went straight to his secretary.

Miss Lilli, write to this Hamilton. You'll find his application documents in the pile on my desk. Tell him to be here next Tuesday. Please wait. The interview with the boss is at 10:30. Write 9:00, 9:00 in my office. That will give me plenty of time to run him through some tests.

Google-rt grinned.

No need to watch a horror movie this week. Next Tuesday, the horror is coming to us.

Maybe there were scarier things. Who knows, Google-rt thought. He wasn't a doctor. Years ago, in an anatomical exhibition, he had once gotten an impression of what nature was capable of.

Google-rt avoided looking at his interlocutor. He sketched a dot next to the other's face while talking to him.

Nice of you to come, Google-rt began the conversation.

The other man, Mr. Hamilton, returned the greeting by thanking him for the invitation.

We have 50 applicants for the position. Hamilton, I'm open, you're one of 50. 2%, if I'm doing my math right.

2% chance of success is better than nothing, replied Hamilton.

We have read your application carefully. There was one point there that we wondered about.

Hamilton remained silent. What was he supposed to say?

There is a three-year gap in your professional career. We wondered what motivated a man like you not to work for three years.

The accident, Hamilton now replied. Actually, it wasn't an accident. It was an illness. I mean injury.

Well, you don't have to talk about it, Google-rt interjected. Curious, he deliberately created an expectant pause.

I have no problem with that. Hamilton straightened up. It was a good job, I mean my

last job before it happened. To be honest, a lot better than the job you are offering.
Google-rt tried to smile. The last sentence was quite a provocation.

On the way to the office, I passed the scene of the accident. An empty house and it was on fire. There were people in front of it, many, very many, I don't remember, they were standing everywhere, shouting, crying, screaming, pushing, but nobody was doing anything. There were enough people, why did I have to stop? Finally, I found out that there was still a child in the house. A boy. His family told me. They had made a fire in the condemned house.

You know, it was automatic. Before I knew it, I was in the smoking building. Burns, Hamilton said. He showed the scars on his hands. His feet had burns too.
He had only been wearing sandals at the time. It had happened in the summer. He pointed to his side.

The side also took a hit. A falling beam. Not pleasant when a wooden lance like that is suddenly stuck in you.
Google-rt understood. The disfigured face was the result of burns.

Did you find the child?

Hamilton nodded.

I'd do it again. Again and again. What are a few scars compared to the life of a child?

I don't mean to offend you, Mr. Hamilton, but you might have saved a potential murderer. Let's say the boy you pulled from the flames goes astray. He kills someone. Maybe even someone in your family.

You mustn't worry, Mr. Google-rt, you mustn't worry when you're helping.

Google-rt looked at the other man's disfigured face for the first time. He couldn't get used to it. His eyes immediately moved to the side again.

Three years, Google-rt said, did it take three years for you to recover?

Hamilton shook his head.

Half a year. Then it was the way it is today. It only cost me my job. It was actually the most important day in my old job. We were about to close a huge deal. My job was to give the presentation in the afternoon and then sign the contracts. My boss told me, Hamilton, you could have saved a million children with that money. You're a fool.

Google-rt became uncomfortable with the conversation.

Let's drop it, Hamilton. I don't want to stir up old things in you again. He handed the other man a folder. The usual tests. We'll see the personnel manager in an hour.

Hamilton opened the folder and began to solve the tasks. Google-rt left the room. He headed straight for the boss's office.

Sir, would you like to take a look at our applicant? I mean, through the window. Don't take it the wrong way, but I'd like to spare you, it may sound strange, I'd like to spare you the sight.

The two of them walked down the corridor into Google-rt's secretary's office. They could see the stranger through a window. Pain and sadness was on his face, ugly crater scars everywhere, scratches, skin bulges, no eyelids.

Forget it, said the HR manager to Googlert. We're not a charity. Let him finish the tests and evaluate them. You know what the test result will be.

Google-rt nodded.

And if he asks about you?

Tell him I have an important appointment, an important appointment has come up. But blame it primarily on the test result. That face! Think about our business customers. Is there a normal spot on his face?

He had no beauty or majesty to attract us to him, nothing in his appearance that we should desire him. He was despised and rejected by mankind, a man of suffering, and familiar with pain. Like one from whom people hide their faces he was despised, and we held him in low esteem. (Isaiah 53:2,3)

Couldn't I at least have a quick word with the personnel manager? Hamilton looked at the other man. You know, it took me a long time to venture out again. And all the rejections. It's the first time I've at least been interviewed. Google-rt shook his head.

I'm sorry, very sorry Mr. Hamilton. We have our principles. And every applicant is treated equally. You have to admit that it's very fair. Hamilton stood up.

Then so be it, he said and left the room in silence.

Google-rt looked after him. The stranger dragged himself outside. Google-rt moved to the window to watch him go. He didn't know why.
There was a dull thud, brief, just a fraction of a second. That Hamilton, why hadn't he seen the truck? He was lying on the road, his disfigured face turned to the sky, his feet and hands exposed, covered in old scars.
A passer-by rushed over. He grabbed Hamilton's side to turn the lifeless body. Blood was seeping from the side of the prostrate body.

Surely, he took up our pain and bore our suffering. But he was pierced for our transgressions, he was crushed for our iniquities. (Isaiah 53:4-5)

Only now did Google-rt see that the truck was carrying iron bars. They lay scattered on the road. Except for one. It had drilled into Hamilton's side.

15.
6+1, A Magic Formula

First day: heaven, earth, light, day, night.
Second day: water below (sea) and water above (sky, clouds).
Third day: separation of the water below from the earth, plants.
Fourth day: sun, moon, stars.
Fifth day: fish, birds.
Sixth day: land animals, human beings.
Seventh day: rest, break.
He had often found it difficult to remember this order. The creation. Why was he thinking about creation? Creation was only positive in the beginning. Although it was separated, land from sea, day from night, it went no further, no dying, no decay, no destruction, only becoming, coming into being, life.
Why did he think of creation? Without it, he would not exist. No worries, no despondency, waves of depressive phases, vain hopes, being at the mercy of others, resignation, they would have been spared all that. And poverty. He

couldn't make a go of it. There had been green branches everywhere since creation, he couldn't find one. Underpaid work, toiling, applying for jobs, nothing, too little, literally too much to die, too little to live.

He sat down in the balmy night and stared at the sky. Covered with clouds. Very few gaps. Ghostly stars. Their light from the infinite vastness. Billions of years on the way. Perhaps the stars no longer existed at all, their light alone the last sign of their former existence. A dream from the past: an astronaut in a silver suit, floating through the black expanse, planets within reach. Kilometers of huge rocks rolling by. No street noise, no post. No telephone. Not a sound. And then, beyond a corner of space, he would see the sky, the heaven with pillars and gold, white-robed beings, people who had already died and others. They would look at him as an astronaut who had managed to get to heaven through the sky.

He stared blankly into the gaps in the night. Waiting for a voice. A light. Sudden thoughts. Something extraordinary. That his life changed abruptly. A different direction. Worry, anger,

hopelessness, vain efforts, poverty, wiped away in an instant.
In vain, no light, no figure, no voice, from afar the last street noise of the day, a single train gliding through the night, a light signal of an airplane flying between the stars, the eternal sound of hundreds of cicadas, a black spider scurrying silently over his bare feet.
I'll draw lots, he thought. It's fairest to me. Draw a lot. Just the drum, where was the lottery drum? The prize? What was the prize? A supervisor? Drawing lots required control, even chance wanted to be controlled.
He got up with difficulty and dragged his depressed body back into the apartment. The worn furniture stared bleakly at him, the same every day, night after night.
Worst of all, the poverty. Others are worse off. A consolation? No, not for him, not for the others.
There had to be a prize in the lottery drum for him. Everyone has a personal prize in the lottery drum of life, despite the many losers. The only thing that was different about this lottery drum was that you could draw as often as you wanted. That seemed to save everything. The big draw

had to come at some point. It was only one side. There were two others. Every thing has two sides, nonsense, the drum of life has three. A big lottery ticket, one side. The freedom to draw an unlimited number of lots, the second side. The many losers, the third side.
Who could guarantee that after the many losses there would be enough strength to survive another one? Wasn't it better to stop drawing at some point? How many people stopped living their lives, just drifting along in their usual daily routine, having given up hope of hitting the jackpot, afraid of drawing another blank.
The lottery drum appeared before his eyes. A fata morgana's distorted image that was constantly deforming, taking on bizarre cubist figures, grimaces, grotesque faces, clowning, within a few seconds. Finally, the image was complete. The round drum had deformed into an angular shape. It took on a third dimension, after all, the lottery drum also had three sides. A book was recognizable. Old, worn and yet not used for a long time, strange letter formations, endless lines with strange life stories that suddenly became visible between the letters.

It was his lottery drum. His problem was shaky poverty, too much to die, too little to live. This lot would end the state of limbo, finally tipping the balance of life, which had been teetering for years, on to one side. How do you use a book as a lottery drum?
I will meditate, he thought, let my thoughts slip into the book. Close my eyes. Then open the book. And look at one place. This place is the lot for which you have waited a long time, not days, not weeks, more than months and years.
He gathered his strength, took the book in his hands, his fingers trembling, and opened it. His eyes refused to rise, a sun that does not want to emerge from the sea in the morning for fear that it is already daytime, that it has become superfluous. A nightmare. Going to sleep at night only to realize the next morning that you have become superfluous – for friends, family, work, for life.
Leave your thoughts, he ordered himself – look at the lot.

Remember the Sabbath day by keeping it holy. Six days you shall labor and do all your work. (Exodus 20:8-9)

After a few minutes, his eyes adjusted and he looked at the words: Remember the Sabbath.
He had never thought of it. This was the front of the lot. A breeze turned the lot to the other side.
Six days you shall labor and do all your work.
Six days you may, he muttered. Was he better than the Creator, who had needed six days for a perfect work? Four days, five days a week. Here was the solution. His lot. Even if it seemed hard, in the end it would be the big one for him.
Six days you shall work. Of course, he thought, I will work for six days, and my life situation will finally lean to one side.
The lot settled on the one bowl of his life and gently pressed it down to him.

16.
Perpetuum petition - Petitioning perpetuum

Solitary, the night moves through the land.
Was he pushy? No, certainly not. Well, he had written 60 petitions so far. 60 petitions, but pushiness was something else. Even if all the petitions were about the same thing. He was right. At least, he was dependent on being heard on this point. If his request was based on this, if the 60 petitions went through, then no-one could speak of being pushy.
The same person always sat on the other side. He had never seen the official. But his name was always written at the bottom. Even after he had turned to the highest authority, the minister, even then, in some small corner of the response there was still the same name of the official with this signature, from which he thought he could read a mixture of aversion, despair, resignation and anger. What might the other person look like? His hair severely parted! Certainly.

Properly dressed, wearing a suit to the office every day, whether it's 10° below zero or 35° at the height of summer. On the left, a huge pile of law books, on the right as well, laws, regulations, executive orders, stacked into a Babylonian tower of a maze of paragraphs. And he was in the middle of it all, lost in the labyrinth of laws and regulations that had obviously been devised just for him. And in front of the official was a folder with his 60 petitions, neatly sorted by date.
Obviously with lots of marginal notes. What he would give to hold these folders in his hands and read the comments. Obviously. Obviously. This word suddenly reminded him of something. The files had to be revealed to him. A revelation, perhaps an oath of disclosure for the officer. Revelation. His mother had prayed. In the past. He had often witnessed it as a child. In the morning, before the day began. Before eating, thanking for the food and asking for a blessing on it. It made sense nowadays, with salmonella, fish tapeworm, pesticides, dioxin, all living and dead additions to food. It made sense to push the food through the filter of prayer before it was consumed.

As a child, he had often seen his mother praying. Then it became rare for a while – he didn't understand why. Was there also an official sitting on the other side when he prayed, as with his petition? Please bless this food.
This request also went into a folder. With a side note: Dear Madam, we can understand your request. But it would be more appropriate for you to contact the farmer who sprays his fruit with pesticides and feeds his cattle with animal meal.
But the official on the other side hadn't sent anything, there was no reply letter in the letterbox the next day and Mother ate the food in good faith. At least his official answered. Although sometimes he would have preferred not to receive a reply.
Suddenly he felt a warm feeling. It was like when his mother used to take him in her arms. His mother was dead, several years dead, yet it was exactly the same feeling when she had held him as a little boy. He was in his mid-40s now, so you don't hug a man like a little boy anymore, even if you are a dead mother. Or so he thought.
But there was no other explanation for the feeling. He felt his eyes drawn to the bookshelf.

At the top, in a corner, was the old family Bible. Leather-bound. Covered in dust and cobwebs.
The feeling pulled him from his chair and he automatically reached for the old book. His fingers left deep imprints in the dust of time.
His hands began to tremble.
What was that all about? Now he was being really childish.
He couldn't suppress the trembling, the book slipped from his grasp and fell to the ground in a huge cloud of dust. When he picked it up, he looked at the open page, curiously reading the words, line by line, faster and faster.
Then he sat down at his desk again, his hands no longer shaking. He took out a sheet of paper and wrote a new petition. Directly to the minister.
His warm feeling told him that he wouldn't have to write many more petitions, perhaps this one would be enough for his request to be granted.
He saw the minister before his eyes as he ran to the official, his last petition in his hand: the minister placed this last petition emphatically on the official's desk:

Grant his request. Finally grant his petitions so that peace can be restored here.

Suppose one of you has a friend to whom he goes to the house at midnight and says, 'Friend, lend me three loaves of bread, because a friend of mine has arrived while I was on my journey, and I have nothing to set before him.' The one inside answers, 'Don't bother me. The door is already shut, and my children are with me in bed. I can't get up and give you anything.' I tell you, though he will not get up and give him anything because he is his friend, yet because of his shameless audacity he will rise and give him as much as he needs. (Luke 11:5-8)

Index

Biography

After graduating from high school in Berlin, I studied medicine in Berlin and Munich and worked in medicine for around 40 years after my studies. I have been retired since the end of 2022. During my professional career I also wrote some manuscripts, a book for young people, children's books, novels and poems. Some have since been self-published.

In addition the author has published several novels in English translation:

Manu's Journey With Death
- A fugue through time

A life, narrated on several levels, accompanied in its tracks and followed by death. In some places, points of this life that have long since passed light up, a brief glowing breath where it pauses for a moment before it is dragged on by the stream of life and disappears somewhere, not without trace but forever. What remains? In any case, death, even if no one is interested in the remnants of this trace of life.

Chrystillian Christmas –
Christmas as usual ~~and~~ different

A goose on its flight to baking-oven land, chasing a golden angel's curl, encountering a mutant Christmas tree, an endless line of waiting stars, Santa's great-great-ancestor and, of course, Father Christmas himself, sitting on a cloud under whose shadow a boy is riding down from the peaks of the Andes, spreading the news of Christ's birth ... It could be like that, but it isn't quite, maybe a little, but just maybe. An Advent calendar of Christmas short stories, profound and loving, varied and multi-faceted, presented in a wonderful narrative style that will enchant even the adult reader. A fragrance-wrapped Christmas soufflé that can be eaten over 26+1 days, on each day of Advent and Christmas plus New Year's Eve, or all at once, depending on the size of your appetite or Christmas taste ...

The Island of Figures
Youth Novel

A little girl in Japan receives a doll from her father for her birthday. When the girl is older, the doll is placed on the waves of the sea in a small boat. Apparently a tradition to mark the transition to a new phase of life into adulthood.
Some time later, another girl travels after her missing doll, and an exciting, adventurous journey begins with an unusual, surprising end.

Roxanna
And the Mysterious Monk

Detective Roxanna has solved her first case when life, or rather death, puts another case on her desk. This brings her into contact with a wealthy English gentleman at his country estate, who has amassed a considerable fortune with an unusual business idea. Among them is a complicated hunter, who is not only a little over-the-top in his language, and especially a monk who, with his incredible intuition, not only beats the inspector to it once.

Roxanna

The Fatal Secret of the Murder Books

It begins with a murder, a somewhat bizarre female detective, events that take place in Rome, England and France. A story that jumps back to the Middle Ages, runs on two tracks, two suspicious women and a dead man who suddenly appears one night to one of the two suspects. A tangled criminal string that seems to have been partially untangled by diligent endeavours – only to become even more tangled in the next moment and finally, seemingly lying in front of you untangled in a perfectly straight line.

Allegories

Short Stories Volume 1 -4

The following collection in 4 volumes contains just over 60 short stories, each short story is based on a biblical passage from the New Testament like a parable and is applied to our time. A short time to catch your breath, a short time perhaps to reflect, a short time perhaps to delve deeper. Although Christ used everyday life for his parables, they still leave a deep impression today. They are easy to remember with a hidden important message that we discover when we think about them.

Uhlenspiegel with the Schilda Citizens

Uhlenspiegel, the lone warrior, armed with an army of mischievous thoughts, encounters a village full of Schilda citizens who are less armed, or rather, armed with different thoughts. Uhlenspiegel's premise: "Where money is at stake, it's good to be good!" And so he mischievously plays out his insights on the Schilda citizens who, with their naive way of thinking, are the appropriate antagonists. Does such an encounter make sense? Amusing and entertaining, in any case!